MW01265574

Ooo Shiny!

Volume 1

Jamie. M. Samland

Meena,
Unicorns are ...
{chef kiss}

Ooo Shiny!

Copyright © 2022 Jamie M. Samland

All rights reserved. No part of this book may be reproduced or used in any manner without the prior written permission of the copyright owner, except for the use of brief quotations in a book review.

Bekaaaaaah!

This was like when we'd text each other shots from the Ikea catalog with a crazy story about the people in it standing beside their Billy bookcases and Ekedalen tables! I turned it into a book!

Cover squirrel by Ryan Allen
@gimble_nackle

What Is This??

You hold in your well-moisturized hands a quick collection of short stories. I kind of ordered them, but the connections between each are tenuous at best; just a shared character, location, or just a concept. What they do all have in common is coming from my brain.

My parents were huge into genealogy when I was a kid. We'd spend "family vacations" in courthouses, looking up birth and death records or in cemeteries searching for the marker of some lost who-knows-what. As a result, when in *Realms of Terswood*, Teiris suggests that she and Daelin go on vacation to the forgotten svarters catacombs, he admits to himself that sounds like fun. Self insert there. Not that I ever *enjoyed* going to cemeteries as a kid, but I've learned to appreciate them. The older, the better. I study the position and condition of markers, and I sleuth out who the people were and what connections they had with each other. Now my motto is "it's not a vacation without going to a graveyard!"

Same thing with this book. I took a tiny idea and

expanded it into something you can read in five to fifteen minutes during your morning constitutional. I'm hoping at least a couple of these will make you grin, maybe even a chuckle, but I'd settle for an eye roll. I reigned myself back from the darkest directions these stories wanted to go, but I still put myself into the mindset of murders more than once. And gnomes.

Enjoy!

And if you do enjoy it, hit my website to get some free stuff!

And if you don't enjoy it, take out your frustration by making a donation to The Trevor Project, Planned Parenthood, or ASPCA.

The Stories and Friends

SEARCHING FOR INSPIRATION

Day eighteen.

Still so many to go.

I stared at the blank screen. With a dark theme in composition mode, only the flashing cursor pierced the void. I noticed my head bobbing with the pulsing line. Was that a second per flash? That seems too fast for a second. I could count ten or fifteen with a timer to know the interval. My hand strayed to my phone where it lay screen-down beside the keyboard, but I caught myself before my fingers flipped it over.

"Do a writing challenge," they said.

"You'll learn so much about your craft," they said.

"It'll be fun," they said.

Thirty short stories in thirty days without creating a list in advance or looking up ideas online. It sounded easy enough. I'm full of ideas. Full of something. I pantsed a full novel that turned out fine enough after the first draft. A short story that takes ten minutes to read might take forty or sixty minutes to draft. Less with an idea already in mind.

I have thirty ideas in me, right? And an hour a day to do what I said I love to do?

The cursor taunted me from the field of black, suggesting otherwise.

Yesterday's tale of a talking sword and the zombies the day before and... what was the day before that... Oh yeah. Another talking sword. Whatever. No one will read any of this; it's just for my own exercise. So what if I repeated a theme?

Wait, that's not a bad idea — repeat myself. That was an exercise I read about somewhere in the stack of books beside my monitor. Write a scene, then a few days later, rewrite it from memory. Maybe change the POV, tell the story from another angle.

My index fingers rested on F and J, rubbing against the nubs, while my thumbs drummed on the spacebar softly enough to not move the flashing cursor.

The flashing, taunting cursor with a growing sense of malevolence.

Which story to rewrite? The one about the aunt's urn? I could write it from the pawnshop owner's perspective. I reached for the glass that was once full of peanut butter-flavored whiskey, now almost empty. What is this type of glass called? Is this a highball? I drank half of what remained. Old-fashioned? Rocks? My phone was in my other hand, already unlocked and prepared to find the answer for me. I tossed it across the room to land on the futon.

Stop, focus. Get something down today and write about another talking sword tomorrow.

My fingers clacked across the keys, creating a pawn shop interior, describing knick-knack and chockeys* and... red squiggly. Chackies*? Chach... screw it, no, don't let a red squiggle stop you. My fingers defined the smell and how the late afternoon light filtered through the dusty air. Dust that was no small portion discarded human skin cells. What did that Facebook clickbait thing say? Something like 80% skin cells? That doesn't seem right.

Gah!

The pawn shop owner came to... comes to life. This will be better in present tense, yeah? I like that. I make a note to go back later and change the lines above. I weave a backstory for him full of an even share of misery and joy. Most of it is just for me, but I try to hint at it with subtle quirks to his demeanor. He's twice divorced, happily married now, but doesn't wear a ring. His kids, by his second wife, are grown and moved out, but they call or at least text a few times a month. Oh, what if he's married to a man now? I grin to myself before rolling my eyes. Not every story has to go queer, as much as I enjoy including the representation. What is this guy's name? Name... name...

My fingers pause their creation and my eyes travel to the book "5,001 Unusual Baby Names" but I manage to control myself from reaching for it.

I look down at the keyboard again and my index fingers pointing to F and J. Fabian, no, Fransisco Jackson.

My fingers set the name in stone and Fransisco, or FJ as his poker buddies call him, now has a mixed heritage. Poker or baccarat? Poker, obvious. Who, other than James Bond, actually plays baccarat. That's not fair. There must be plenty of baccarat players in the world. Where did I set this story? I remember the clear image of the character leaving the pawn shop and how I imagine an Arizona strip mall would look.

My fingers itch to research baccarat clubs in urban Arizona — Scottsdale maybe? — but I force them instead to focus on what task FJ was in the middle of when the unnamed protagonist entered with the chime of the old bell suspended on a spring over the door. Was there a bell? Was it a buzzer? Was there nothing specified and thus left to the reader's imagination? What reader?

I finish my whiskey with a frown, knowing it took me an entire glass to transcribe a thousand words from my mind as that blasted, flashing cursor slowly navigated across the screen and snapped back to the left. A thousand? No, surely that's twelve or fourteen hundred. I still had two-thirds of the story to write. Haggling for and buying the urn, then discovering it still contained cremains. FJ started as nothing and was now a living, breathing person with his own hopes and fears and bulk warehouse membership. I like FJ and wonder what other stories would come through his shop. His stories would be like Deep Space Nine, where the adventure comes to him. What other quirky shop owners lease space in his strip mall? What is the landlord like? What if there's a treasure map hidden in the urn? Or a ghost?

I hit enter a few times and brainstorm what other hijinks might happen to FJ, grinning wider with each bullet point. Finally, I look at the paragraphs above and highlight them.

"298 of 411 words"

The red squiggle below "chockeys*" taunts me.

GOBLIN ASSAULT

Trevor breathed out and steadied his aim. The bowstring twanged by his ear, and the arrow flew true. The goblin grabbed at the shaft protruding from its shoulder and fell from the makeshift ladder, crashing into and knocking off the one behind it.

"There're too many of them!" Trevor nocked again and readied his aim. The ranger's arrows always flew true, and this was no exception as it hit the next goblin in the center of its chest.

"Protect the crystal!" Caleb yelled and clashed swords with the goblins that flooded over the railing on the far side of the sanctuary. He parried and pushed, getting a foot up to kick the green-skinned beast back. It screamed, a shrill scraping noise, as it fell to a messy death a hundred feet below. "Raaji! We need that protection spell!"

The third of their band knelt in the center of the Forest Sanctuary, hovering over the Sacred Crystal of the North Forest. Raaji arranged the arcane dusts, twigs, and gleaming gems that provided the power of his art. "I'm almost there!" he shouted back. Despite the concentration his work required, he aimed a shot of fire at the back of a goblin as it ran at Caleb's back. It exploded across the creature's flank to throw it screaming off the platform's edge. Raaji closed his eyes and called to the ancient spirits of the forest that clung to this divine place. They were slow to respond, content to remain in their quiet slumber, but his Will overpowered their desire to remain at rest and his hands radiated soft, blue light as he waved them over his artifacts.

"I'm out of arrows!" Trevor bellowed and swung his bow like a staff, knocking back each goblin as they surged forward.

"Ah! They got me!" Caleb dropped to a knee and held his leg, blood pouring around his fingers. A goblin raised his sword, preparing to land the final blow and end one of the three protectors of the forest. Caleb's fingers clasped the hilt of his father's dagger hidden in his boot and held his breath, awaiting the moment to strike.

A flash of white shot through the goblin's chest. It looked down with confusion, stumbled back, and toppled off the platform.

"What was that?" Caleb shot to his feet.

"A magic arrow," Trevor said and, for emphasis, shot another into a goblin as it swung over the top of the ladder.

"You said you were out," said Caleb.

"Yeah, but I have magic arrows, too."

"Since when?"

"I killed enough goblins. I learned a new power."

"You can't level up in the middle of a battle, Trevor."

"I have cast the spell," Raaji announced from the center of the platform. A soft golden white washed over the three harmlessly and destroyed the few remaining goblins. "The crystal is safe!"

"Trevor cheated," Caleb huffed and tossed down his sword.

"No, I didn't!" Trevor raised his bow, and a glistening arrow appeared between his fingers as he pulled back the string aimed at his comrade.

"You can't shoot me. The battle's over."

"You guys suck." Trevor threw down his bow and descended the ladder he'd been defending.

"Boys!" the Warden of the Forest called to them from the distance. "Dinner time!"

MR BROWN

Sunlight streamed through the floor-to-cathedral-ceiling windows that provided a breathtaking view of Versailles to the south and Paris to the east. On a clear day, much like today, one could squint and make out the tip of the Eiffel Tower from this height. Today, that sunshine reflected off the still-wet pool of blood on the kitchen floor. Mr. Brown knelt to take the fridge magnet from where it pierced the throat of the venerable Bishop Blanc. He wiped a thumb across the slick blood and grinned at the text printed in white against a rainbow background, "Always be yourself. Unless you can be a unicorn. Then always be a unicorn!" Mr. Brown cast an eye across the late bishop's high-rise apartment, decorated in tasteful, artistic bursts of colors in the form of Monets, Cézannes, two Modigliani sculptures, and a da Vinci diary under a glass case. Mr. Brown shook his head and grinned. Whoever funded his visit to the late bishop's apartment this afternoon possessed the connections to end a man with this wealth and influence. News of Bishop Blanc's sudden death, leader of the Neo-Catholic movement, anti-Christ or Christ-reborn, depending on which side of the French-Italian border you preferred, would rock the world, believer or not. Everything would change when the unfortunate maid came at 6pm sharp.

Or it might not. The Church may just as well invent a different truth. It really all depended on which side got here first. Mr. Brown didn't care so long as the proverbial paychecks continued to clear.

Mr. Brown wiped his hands on a dish towel before folding it neatly over the oven's handle, put the magnet on the stainless steel Bluetooth-enabled refrigerator, and exited the apartment. He took out his phone and opened the app with a cutesy cartoon garrote wire icon. When he checked the "Complete!" box, the contract faded to be replaced with another. He looked at the app once more before tucking away his phone and walking to the art déco-inspired elevator. As the muzak played a royalty-free version of 1992's smash hit "The Sign," Mr. Brown mouthed the words.

"Why do I bother when you're not the one for me?" He circled his hips. "Oo-oooo-oo."

Ding!

As he strolled across the lobby of deep, rich woods and tastefully manicured plants, Mr. Brown considered the logistics needed to deliver him to eastern Austria for the next contract and wished for the dozenth time that the app developers would listen to feedback and allow for location-based job searches. Outside, the doorman hailed a cab for him and directed the driver to the nearest train station.

The next job awaits.

IVAN'S LIBRARY

I hate being sent to the basement, but as the newest employee of the Red Square Krispy Kreme, there's no one else for me to defer to. Why the manager stored the sacks of unconstituted glaze in the farthest, darkest corner when it's a material used in literally every batch of donuts is a mystery to me. I flicked on the switch at the bottom of the steps, but the 25 watts of incandescence was barely enough to guide my way through the mess. I passed through the narrow shelves and pulled a wooden torch from the sconce at the bulb's farthest reach. Taking an old Bic lighter from my pocket, I fumbled at the flint wheel until the spark was enough to bring the brand to life.

Passing into the warren of storage tunnels, I grumbled again, pleading to god that someone else would be hired next week and this would be my last trip down here. Not that I could quit. As a third-year university student majoring in ancient literacy, Krispy Kreme likely held more lucrative job offerings than my eventual degree would. I pulled the crumpled map on a napkin from my pocket and held it to the torch's sputtering light. "Left at the altar, left at the second mausoleum, right at the third unexploded munitions cache" Yeah, yeah, left, left, right. I'd made this trip enough times; I should know the way. I pushed the map back into my pocket and continued forward.

I paused for a breath at the altar. Carved of a single piece of obsidian, the cloaked nun, almost as tall as me, held a plate for offerings. There was usually a bag of white mushroom chips or a bottle of Baykal. Today, it was a plate of salted herring and onions beside a stuffed bear. I shrugged and moved on to the left.

One mausoleum, two mausoleums, left again.

I moved the torch to my left hand, farther from the first cache of unexploded munitions as I passed it. I began doubting myself with each step. Was it the second or third cache? 1-2-3 sounded right, but as I stood beside the next pile of large steel casings, the path to the right looked so familiar. I pulled the napkin from my pocket and held it to the torch's light. The lines and letters were smudged, and I moved it closer — And dropped the napkin with a shout as it burst into flames.

I cursed the Krispy Kreme regional manager.

I'd already been in the basement long enough and knew my team lead would yell at me when I returned. I sighed and turned right. If it was wrong, I'd just come back and go to the next cache.

After a few steps, the tunnel was less familiar, but just as I was about to turn around, I saw the sacks of glaze ahead, reflecting off my torchlight. Taking back my curse, I picked up a sack, noticing the layer of dust on it and the four others in the small, square dead end. This wasn't right. There should be a hall continuing to the catacombs under the Kremlin. No time to worry about this right now; I can't get fired. I turned to leave, but the torchlight glinted off a gold panel on the wall.

Sighing, I dropped the sack and touched the panel. It pushed in easily, and the other sacks of unconstituted glaze fell in as a hidden door they leaned against slid open. A rush of stale air smelling of moldering parchment wafted past, and I stepped into the cool chamber beyond. My torch was worthless in the space, but I could tell by the acoustics I stood on a catwalk overlooking a cavernous room. For the first time in my life, my university studies came into real-life practice as I read the old Cyrillic script popular in the 1500s.

"Welcome to Ivan's Golden Library! Please enjoy your stay!"

I groaned. I'm so getting fired.

GREAT-AUNT IDA

I raised my face to the sun as the jingle of the pawnshop door faded behind me. A warm breeze carried with it the first hints of spring: the dirt and bacteria of petrichor mixed with well-meaning blossoms. My hand brushed over the pocket bulging with tens and twenties. Well, more tens than twenties. One twenty and three tens…. But enough for a reasonable dinner, as long as Neil didn't want a drink with it. That was an easy enough fix. I'll suggest a vodka and Dew before we leave the apartment. I crossed the parking lot, cracked and dotted with vibrant yellow dandelions, and leaned against the bus stop shelter. My eyes automatically scanned the decals of bands long broken up and a flier for piano lessons and tattoos, both at the same number.

The bus hissed to a stop, I swiped my card, and took the first open seat. The bills in my pocket called for attention again, and I spared a glance back to the run-down strip mall just as the bus turned the first corner. Something nagged in the back of my mind. Regret? Shame? No, my apartment was small, too small for the fireplace that took up half the living room and too small for the gaudy blue and gold vase that took up half the mantle. Half and half; that thing took up a quarter of the room. No one could fault me for tidying up my life and bringing my own style into my living. Marie Kondo would be proud. The old vase, always loud and proud on mom's fireplace and until this morning, mine, never sparked joy. Now I'd get a mediocre steak dinner out of it.

Still, my mind looked back to the sad little pawn shop full of sad little discarded crap. A smile slid across my lips. Mom always described her great-aunt Ida's house that way, bursting with worthless trinkets and collectibles, musty with a coat of dust over things that hadn't been touched or thought about in a decade. I never met great-aunt Ida, but I imagined I'd be stuck going to her house for long, terrible summer afternoons, sharing the time with equally terrible second cousins that, other than being around my age, I had nothing in common with.

I hoped the pawnshop owner did something with great-aunt Ida before reselling the vase.

AS BEST HE COULD

The deep stench of ancient decay and moldering fabric stung Gerold's nose. Well, it would if he still had a nose. That fell off years ago. Decades? Who knows. It was hard to remember with a brain mostly eaten by mice. Whatever force allowed him to think also gave him sight without eyes. He watched through the single crack in the stone as a procession passed him with their faces downcast and shrouded behind veils. They sang a slow dirge in a language Gerold vaguely remembered. He shifted closer to the wall and tried to call out as their light and song were lost around a corner.

Gerold sighed as best he could and flopped away from the cracks to lie in the complete darkness. He drummed bony fingers over his ribs, tapping out the dirge tune and using his spine for the bass notes. He felt a tug deep in his chest and shooed away the giant rat trying to make off with the bit of organ still there. Other than a bit of brains, it was all the fleshy bits Gerold had remaining, and he protected it fiercely.

People were talking, and Gerold spun back to the crack. He heard hushed tones in an accent and dialect so thick it strained Gerold's mice-eaten brains to understand.

"The last of the Dark One's minions have been destroyed," said one and stopped just be front of the wall. "Sir Unur slew the last lich lord in the east."

"Brilliant news, excellent," said the second. "I never imagined I would feel relief to be in the catacombs, not after fighting the undead since the time of our great-great-grandsires."

The first laughed. "I understand the sentiment, but the royal catacombs were the first to be cleansed when the Dark One spread his foul magics and raised the dead a hundred years ago. All the risen here were put down ages ago."

Gerold frowned as best he could. He seemed to remember men in shiny armor rushing by, brandishing relics as bright as the sun. What small amount of that light that made it through the crack in the wall had hurt, but it hadn't been that much. Back then, Gerold was driven by a desire to get at those men and... and... rip them to bloody shreds in the name of the Dark One, the true master of this world that would herald its end. No, that couldn't be right. Gerold didn't want to hurt anyone. Even the rat that wanted so badly to eat his last fleshy bit, he just shooed that away. Though... He'd always been kind to the rats and mice. It had only been recently that his thirst for human suffering had abated.

Gerold tried to make a sound at the men, but that was long ago impossible. He tapped at his ribs, but he heard that as the vibration traveled through his bones, rather than a sound in the air. He took the massive gold ring from his left hand and pushed it through the crack in the wall. For a moment, he worried it was stuck until it fell free with a sharp clatter between the speakers.

"What is..." one started, and Gerold saw a fleshy hand take the ring. "It's a royal signet. How did this get here?"

They murmured back and forth for a minute in breathy voices too low for Gerold to make out before darting away and taking their torchlight with them.

Gerold laid back and cursed as best he could. While he was distracted by the pair speaking about a Dark One and undead, the rat made off with his last fleshy bit.

Time meant little when the infrequent funeral procession was the only way to tell its passing.

Gerold found himself missing the rats that left him alone, now with no fleshy bits, and he wondered why the mice weren't coming back for the rest of his brains. Was something wrong with the brains he had left? What if he had no brains left and only thought he did? He couldn't very well look inside his head.

Finally, torchlight shone through the crack, along with shouted orders. Something crashed against the wall, again and again, until the light flooded in as stones were removed one after another. The light was almost touching Gerold when he heard a gasp, and the work paused.

"This is the tomb of King Gerold XII! He united the outer islands two hundred years ago and was arguably our greatest king! Take the utmost care!"

The stones were being removed again, but more slowly.

Gerold froze. In the increased light, he looked back to the sarcophagus he'd crawled out of ages ago and again frowned the best he could. These people revered him. If he acted like a normal skeleton was expected to act, they would gather up the bones he'd scattered over the years. That would be nice. He lost his legs and pelvis coming out of the stone coffin. Then they would place him with the dearest reverence back in here, to spend all eternity in total darkness. No dirges to drum along with, no mice to shoo away.

The first light in centuries touched Gerold, the first light to ever touch his bare ribs. A bearded face poked through the hole in the wall and gasped with an excited little sound. Another few moments and Gerold was fully in the light, still unmoving.

"It's really him," the scholar said and knelt beside him before glancing at the empty sarcophagus. "He must have been risen by the Dark One's call and trapped back here. He returned to his eternal rest as Sir Unur defeated the last minion of that foul monster. Come, let us clean up the king's vestments and place him again to rest."

Gerold frowned as best he could. He couldn't spend forever in a box. Only one other option.

He raised an arm and waved.

STARVING

"Is anyone else, like, starving all of a sudden?"

"You're always hungry, Kimmy," said Andre with a chuckle. "But yeah, now that you mention it, I wouldn't mind stopping for a bite to eat."

"I have cage-free turkey jerky," said Pat and set down their pack beside the other two.

"While that sounds nice," said Kimmy, "I hope you realize that turkey cages would have to be huge. That's just a marketing ploy to pull at your sympathetic strings."

Pat looked up from where they squatted in front of their bag. "Hey, if you saw two boxes of cereal and one said 'asbestos free' and the other didn't, which would you buy?"

"Ha!" Andre chuckled as he accepted a salted meat stick. "Good point, babe." He leaned back against a twisted oak and watched the sky through the gaps in the canopy. "It'll get dark soon. What if we camped right here?"

"Maybe not a bad idea." Kimmy looked up from her map and compass. "We made pretty good progress today. I think we're within twenty miles of the dock. Most of that will be downhill, but that's more than I have left in me today. Won't be a problem for tomorrow. There should be a stream..." She spun a slow circle with the map in one hand. "That way in about a hundred feet, maybe less. I'll go get us water." She gathered up the jugs and left.

"Alone at last," said Andre and pushed off the tree with his best sexy walk.

"Oh, that is so not going to happen. Not tonight, at least." Pat winked and loosened the straps holding the tents to their pack.

"So you're saying it is going to happen?" Andre waggled his eyebrows.

Pat rolled their eyes. "I'm married to an idiot. I should have listened to my mother seven years ago."

"Is this too much? Did your momma warn you against all this?" Andre continued his sexy dance, touching his nipples through his shirt with a wide grin across his sunburnt face while he bit his lower lip.

A scream pierced the evening.

"Kimmy!" Pat shouted, and they both took off at a run through the tangle of undergrowth, jumping over fallen logs and knocking aside branches as they dashed after their friend. They found the stream quickly enough with Kimmy beside it, pushed against a tree with both hands covering her mouth and eyes wide with fright. Pat ran to her, putting their palms on her shoulders, while Andre scrambled to collect the water jugs before they washed away in the slow stream.

"Kimmy, what's wrong?" Pat asked.

Kimmy blinked twice and shook her head before gesturing past Pat with her chin. "It startled me."

Pat followed her gaze and clapped a hand over their mouth to hold in the gasp of shock. Across the stream, atop a thick wooden stake and looped with beads, were two human skulls.

"Is she okay? What--" Andre looked across the stream and shrieked.

"We can't stay here!" said Kimmy. "There are cannibals or something on this island!"

Pat exhaled a deep breath and stepped into the water, closer to the impaled heads. "They're decades old, maybe older. That true-crime podcast said it takes like fifty years for all the skin to fall off. Though, who knows with the conditions on the island. Point is, this isn't new, and the rangers would have known about an indigenous tribe here."

"We should get back to our packs," Andre said

without taking his eyes off the stake and heads.

A moment later, they were back at their bags and the mess created by a hasty departure.

"Despite that," Kimmy said and waved back toward the stream and the horror there, "I'm still like super hungry."

"Yeah, me too," Andre agreed. "What do we have left, babe?"

Pat put out a tarp and dumped their pack. Trail bars, jerky, snack packs of nuts, sandwich bags of rice and chopped peppers. The three grabbed at the food and devoured it, but their stomachs still growled, wanting more.

"One would think," said Andre as he ate rice from a ziplock like a horse with a feedbag, "that seeing a couple of rotted, severed heads would reduce one's appetite. But damn if it didn't make me more hungry."

They shared a collective chuckle and eyed the last piece of cage-free turkey jerky.

"Split it?" Kimmy offered and tore it in thirds. Andre licked his lips as he accepted his portion.

"I'm still starving," Andre moaned and Pat dug through their packs to confirm nothing else edible lurked in the bottoms. "If I were a cannibal, I'd eat you first, Kimmy."

She laughed and pushed away his chomping

advances. "Shut up! You're so stupid."

Kimmy had her own tent for the last four nights of their hike across the island, but the three unanimously decided to squeeze into a single tent for the last night, too hungry and tired to set up the second. As they lay in the tent's warmth, only the crickets and other night insects buzzed, audible around the growling of their stomachs.

* * *

Ranger Smitts reviewed the ferry manifest with a frown. Seven came last week and only four left. "Great," she grumbled, "probably high on shrooms staring at a waterfall. Or..." She considered a stray idea, but shook her head.

"Or legitimately in need of help," offered Junior Ranger King. "We have to find them all the same."

"Yeah, no shit. Come on."

Find them, they did. Just under twenty miles from the ranger's station, Smitts and King saw the bright orange tent through the trees. Three packs were upended nearby, with wrappers and garbage strewn across the makeshift campsite.

Smitts put a hand on the butt of her service pistol and nodded to the tent's flap. "Open it."

King crept close and reached trembling fingers

for the zipper. He screamed and fell back when he saw what lay within. Still in their nightclothes, three skeletons lay, picked clean in the tight tent.

"Jesus..." Smitts moaned. "Not again."

D.E.D. MIXER

"Hurry up, Todd! We'll be late!" I shouted back at my zombie, but nothing could rush his shambling gait. What started as a senior project and practical essay ended in a permanently raised zombie and the reason why I could never get anywhere on time. I know, nothing revolutionary there. A zombie, big whoop. But at nineteen, my teachers all applauded my scholastic application.

As all in my line of craft are warned early on, don't get attached to your work. Well, I did and two years later, Todd still followed me everywhere. I couldn't leave him at home or he'd bump into a wall all day trying to get to me. I certainly couldn't bring myself to take him to one of the conjuration majors to have them, you know, take Todd to a farm upstate. Instead, I had him registered with the school as an ongoing thesis research project and emotional support zombie.

"Hey Emmit!"

I looked up at Charlotte Conners waving and gliding toward me on a puffy cloud. A bundle of textbooks hovered in the air beside her.

I waved back with a grin. "Hey Char. That's a fancy way to get around." I gestured at her cloud.

"It's just an illusion." She lifted each leg from the cloud to prove she wasn't standing on it. "It's a total pain in the ass to maintain. I have to use this five hours a day for the next week. I don't see how this has anything to do with an evocation degree. Stupid electives."

I looked back at Todd and sighed. He stood at a step and stared down in utter confusion. Charlotte glided beside me as I stomped toward my zombie. "You still have Todd? My roommate is taking a 400-level course for cleanses and cures. I'm sure she'd be happy to take a look at him for you."

"Thanks, but I'm holding on to him for a longer project now." I stepped beside Todd and he looked up at me with milky, expectant eyes. I couldn't help but crack a smile at him. Stepping onto the grass, I went up the hill beside the pavement and Todd followed.

"Hey, a bunch of us are having a mixer at the Delta Epsilon Delta house tonight. You should totally come." She held out a bright yellow photocopied invitation covered with fun, arcane symbols.

"Thanks, Char, but I'll be pretty busy today."

She frowned. "You're always busy, Emmit."

The bell rang behind us.

"Crap, sorry Emmit, I gotta get to class." She pressed the invitation toward me. "I hope to see you later!"

"C'ya, Char." I folded the invitation and stuffed it into a pocket. Grabbing Todd by the wrist, I pulled him after me as I rushed us toward the building. "Am I going to have to find some new legs for you?"

Classes droned on in the warmth of early spring. Magic Requirements continued a lesson on calculating exact mana requirements for ritual spells, hence the name of the class. I didn't see the use in knowing that unless mana was limited for some reason, but I took notes all the same. Todd gently moaned beside me during Lich History and I shooed him away as I practiced Minor Cure and Lesser Regeneration in my abjuration elective.

The sun barely peeked over the stately trees lining the campus as I strolled back toward the dorms.

"Emmit!"

I recognized the voice calling out and cringed. Todd Smenk jogged toward me, flanked by his cronies, Gasper and Jasper.

"Hey you still got this stupid zombie?" asked

the living Todd, and poked the undead one in the chest. Todd the zombie looked down at the finger, then at me with milky eyes that seemed to ask permission.

"Leave him alone, Todd," I grumbled.

"Hey Gasper, Jasper, you know he named his zombie after me? I think Emmit has a crush on me. Do you kiss him at night and pretend it's me?"

"You wish, Todd." I wanted him gone. Todd Smenk came out of nowhere one day last year to harass me and never stopped. I wracked my brain at the beginning, wondering what I could have possibly done to warrant it, but I never came up with anything. Living Todd cycled between six veins of teasing and I imagined he had a wheel at home that he spun to decide which he'd stick to each day. Today he landed on, "Tease Emmit that his zombie's name implies latent homosexuality and a desire to possess me." Nothing latent about it, but that's not his damned business.

"Go back to your summoned imps and lesser demons, Todd. Maybe one of them will love you, unlike your father." Harsh, but a year of snide comments had me at a breaking point.

The smirk on Living Todd's ugly, freckled face melted to a scowl. "Screw you, Emmit. Go home and screw your damn zombie." He spat at my feet and whirled away, trailed by his goons.

I bit my lip to keep from smiling as I watched them retreat. I know we weren't supposed to use magic against other students, but using a little divination to pry out one of Living Todd's deepest insecurities was nothing more than a practical application, right?

Back in my dorm room, Todd went to his corner and stood there, facing me on my bed and swaying slightly. My roommate, a senior enchantment major was, as usual, not in. I think he'd slept three nights in his own bed all year. Before then, I wouldn't have guessed someone focusing their studies on controlling others' minds would end up spending every night in someone else's bed.

I piled my books on the desk and pulled off my heavy school of necromancy cloak. As I sat down to read a chapter about Om'quenur IIX, fabled lich lord of the fourth century, Todd started moaning in the corner. I hushed him, but he continued.

When the moaning got louder than the voice reading in my head, I slammed my palm on the desk and jerked around to my zombie. "What, Todd? What do you want?"

He held out a bright yellow piece of folded paper.

"No, Todd. I really have to study tonight. If I can't remember the succession of Dark Lords through the Bozok Dynasty, I'm going to fail the exam tomorrow."

His moan lessened to a whine and a whimper. I groaned and slammed my textbook closed. "Fine, Todd. We'll go for like an hour, then I have to get back." He stopped moaning and stood a little straighter.

I pulled on my skull hoodie and black jeans before taking a moment in front of the mirror to ensure my hair was adequately messed up. I knew full well that certain stereotypes existed between the different schools of magic and knew I fell deep into what a necromancy major was expected to look like. I didn't care. Hoodies and tight jeans were comfortable.

I looked over at Todd and tugged a black skull beanie around his ears.

The walk to Delta Epsilon Delta only took fifteen minutes. Eight, were I able to leave Todd at home. I helped him over the curbs and marveled up at the stately sorority house with D.E.D. clear in embossed carvings in the stone over the wide front doors. The soft thump of music hurried my feet, and I remembered my promise to Todd: only one hour, then back to studying. Mounting the steps, I raised my arm to knock, but the door opened to a grinning Charlotte Conners wearing an oversized sweatshirt and possibly no pants. A small party raged on behind her,

"Emmit, you made it!" She looked past me to Todd, struggling with the bottom step. "Sorry, familiars aren't allowed in the house, but you can leave him around back." She waved around the right side of the property. "Hurry back, Shanta is about to show us some kinky ways to use telekinesis." Charlotte winked and closed the door in my face.

I swallowed the lump in my throat and turned to Todd. Why in the greater hells did Charlotte Conners want me at this party? Awkward Emmit, that my classmates befriended only if they needed a tutor, but otherwise were too busy to call. I seriously considered going back home and forgetting the whole thing, but found my legs taking me around the back of the house. What would they have to hold familiars, a pit they expected me to drop Todd into and run inside? That sounded cruel.

Two zombies, a cat, and three ravens stood or sat idly in a knee-high pen by the sorority's backdoor. A guy wearing a white hoodie, pants, and matching hair looked up from his book,

Traitors and White. I'd heard about that book; saw a lot of the girls reading it under their desks in class or out on the lawns. It was supposed to be some really steamy stuff. He grinned at me, but that faded when he saw Todd.

"Dropping off your zombie so you can join the party?" he asked and closed his book with a finger to mark the page.

"I guess so. What keeps the ravens and cats from escaping?"

"Me." He tapped the narrow gate on the pen and I noticed the faint pulse of white around its perimeter as he opened it.

I pointed for Todd to shamble into the enclosure, and the guy in white locked it.

"That's a neat trick," I said. "Abjuration?"

He gestured to his clothes. "What gave it away?"

"Would you guess I'm a necromancy student?" I picked at my black skull hoodie with a grin.

"Necromancy? With a zombie and wearing all black? I would have put money on divination." A smile flicked across his face with a light chuckle. "You should get inside. The sweet party awaits."

I started to reflexively turn with the dismissal, but caught myself. "Hey, uh, I'm Emmit. Emmit Metus." I extended a hand.

"Metus? Like, Latin for fear? You must be from a line of necromancers." He took my hand in a firm grip.

"It used to be longer, but they made them change it when coming into the country."

"As they do, sure. Mine's no better. Virgil Spes. Pleasure to meet you, Emmit." Virgil chewed his lip and tapped on his book's cover, as if waiting for me to add to the conversation.

"I'm taking an abjuration elective," I blurted without knowing why.

"That's good. Good to study your opposites for a well-rounded education."

The thump of the party's music continued. I glanced up at Virgil's pale blue eyes with a grin, then nodded down at his book. "I haven't seen any guys reading that. I thought it was for girls." As soon as my words came out, I cringed. "I mean I—"

"What about a book genders the audience, Emmit?"

"I mean, I've only seen girls reading it."

"Just keep digging that hole, buddy. Insert necromancy joke here."

"I'm sorry." I looked down at my shoes for a moment and was surprised by Virgil's smile when I looked back up at him.

"I'm just screwing with you. I don't really care. It's a well-told story set across six generations with complex social and political weavings, but I read it for the hot sex scenes." He raised the book and tapped the cover again. "I mean, *really* hot sex scenes."

I glanced at the post nearest to Virgil and wanted to sit down to talk with him, but a burst of laughter from within the house pulled both our attentions.

"Shouldn't you be getting to your party, Emmit Metus?" Virgil asked and looked over me in a way that would normally leave me feeling uncomfortable and shrink away. Coming from this stranger in white, a little burst of confidence blossomed within me.

"I don't know why they invited me," I said. "Probably to do someone's homework or to do weird magic experiments on."

"At least you were invited, though I'm not sure I'd come if they asked me."

I recognized the little flutter in my belly. I was crushing on this guy. Polar opposite by study, but linked by being social outcasts. His well-groomed, snowy hair, ear studs, and white-painted nails all added to my interest.

"Hey, weird question," I said and couldn't stop

the words that came next. "Do you want to get out of here? Get some coffee?"

Virgil tapped the sexy book on his lips. "Definitely."

The butterflies in my gut exploded in some new evolution and I'm sure my smile made me look like an idiot. I called for Todd to come back to the gate.

"Sorry," said Virgil. "I didn't mean right now this very second. I'm sort of on the clock." He gestured at the pen of familiars.

"Oh yeah, yeah," I laughed to hide the awkwardness. Todd arrived at the gate and Virgil unlocked it to let him pass.

"We'll get that coffee real soon, Emmit Metus." Virgil looked me over again and winked.

"Do you want to exchange info or..."

"Divination minor," Virgil said, and tapped the side of his head. "I know how to find you and enough to know we'll have fun." He winked again.

I waved and took a few steps backward with Todd at my side, trying to decide if I was flattered or angry at having divination spells secretly cast upon me while I awkwardly flirted with a boy. A few hours ago, I did the same thing to Living Todd. I settled on somewhere closer to flattered as the smile never faded during the fifteen minutes back to my dorm, the hours studying lich lord legacies, or as I lie in bed, trying in vain to fall asleep, but thinking of a boy with a sexy book.

GLITTERBOMB

The towering stacks belched smoke, choking the evening sky. In the shadow of the stacks was nestled a pub carved from an overgrown mushroom. Within the pub, a dozen gnomes sat apart on their stools, contemplating frothy ales after a long day on their feet. Not all the gnomes drank alone. In fact, two sat beside each other in animated conversation.

"Ug, I'm still covered in glitter," Nesybar complained and brushed at his arms.

"Don't touch it; it'll just spread," said Ronxif, waving for his brother to stop touching himself. "That's what you get for working where you do."

Nesybar shot a scathing look. "So sorry I can't work in a bird-flippin' garden all day, standing around, doing gosh darn nothing."

"Hey!" Ronxif glanced around nervously at the other patrons sitting on their soft cap stools. "There's no need to use that kind of language. I can probably still get you a job, but you'd have to start out in an entry-level position."

Nesybar leaned back and crossed his arms. "I'm perfectly fine at the plant. I don't need your handouts."

"Oh come on, brother. Don't think of it like that. Being a garden gnome is in our blood! I work beside four generations of our people every day. You can't really be happy working at a meat packing plant. What do you even do there? I can't imagine they have any machinery that a gnome could use."

"Ogrora Farms have made several important advancements in the last few years and are one of the empire's top employers of mythical and magic creatures. We can get proper jobs now, Ronxif. We're not bound by the same racial bias and constraints as our father and his before."

"You sound like a commercial, sheesh." Ronxif lifted his mug of mead and turned back toward the bar.

"I'm chief inspector of final product."

"So you look over all the meat before it goes out on trucks? The faery meat? No wonder you're always covered in glitter."

"If you knew how many contaminants there are in faery meat, you would be shocked. They bring a faery in, looks fine. Slaughter it and take it through the selection lines, still looks fine. But once it's under cellophane and particular lighting, only then can you see the faery was cursed. I end up rejecting a full quarter of product and you should be glad that isn't making it to market."

Ronxif eyed the breaded and fried faerysticks in front of him with suspicion. "Oh gosh, what do you do with the rejects?"

"It's all incinerated by the end of the day."

"Well, if you can get an only slightly cursed faery short loin or ribs cheap, see if you send it my way. My anniversary is coming up, and I'd love to surprise Vosany with a home-cooked faery rib and baked mushroom dinner."

"Well," Nesybar glanced around the bar and nudged closer to his brother. "You didn't hear it from me, but Ogrora Farms is about to start a new product line. I asked you for drinks because I wanted to tell you I'm getting promoted to senior chief inspector and transferred off the faery line."

"New product?" Ronxif gasped and grabbed his brother by the elbows. "Is it bugbear? I've always wanted to taste bugbear, but I hear they're borderline sentient and that's, like, frowned upon. Basilisk?"

Nesybar grinned and waggled his eyebrows.

"Kraken?"

"Better," Nesybar said, and lowered his voice to

a breathy whisper. "We're getting into unicorn."

Ronxif's eyes went wide with another gasp. "No way."

"Way."

"Wow, bro, I'm happy for you. That'll be fun! But," Ronxif chuckled. "You'll meet me in the bar covered in rainbows instead of glitter."

They both laughed and clacked their mugs together in a toast.

POPUP

I touched my temple to start recording, peeked in the door, and almost fell over. She lay across the bed, all legs and curves, barely covered by the silky sheets. Her skin glimmered in the dim light of the oil lamp on the davenport. Her long hair, black as a raven's wing, cascaded around her... her... I swallowed hard. It took all my nerve to not run, but my brother paid for me to be here, saying I'd leave a man. I wanted to be a man. He just wanted to watch my recording afterward. Creep. I rubbed my chest where he'd punched me and entered the room.

She shifted, sitting up straighter and holding the blanket loosely to her chest. My eyes sought the floor, but nothing could stop the involuntary twitch to her perfect lips, those thighs.

"Don't be nervous," she said, and I barely noticed the odd cadence in her voice.

My legs almost gave out twice as I inched toward the bed.

I was horribly nervous, but it didn't matter for

long and I left, according to my brother, a man.

He was supposed to pick me up, but the brothel parking lot was empty, save for two old hovercars. In his defense, he paid for an hour and I was out really early. I stood there for a moment and watched my recording again. Images of the motbot's creamy legs overlaid the depressing park lot. I quickly edited out what I wouldn't want my brother to see and looped a few parts to lengthen the playback. As I did, I noticed a void at the bottom of the recording, like a bar that took up a full fifth of my vision. I archived the files, keeping the original safe in a private drive, and closed the recording.

The black void across the bottom of my vision remained.

"Want to meet hot babes in your area?" said a sultry voice behind me. I whirled to a busty girl barely wearing a school girl's outfit. She leaned toward me, flickered, and disappeared. Text scrolled across the void at the bottom of my vision, repeating her question with a web link.

Two topless girls were making out to my left, link below. A woman older than my grandmother played with the tassels on her nipples, link below. Three other girls that looked younger than me blinked their long lashes with wolfish innocence.

Link.

I dropped to my knees with a scream and shut down my ocular implants. The world went dark and silent, save for the buzz from the parking lot lamps. I counted nine minutes and forty seconds before I heard my brother's Chrysler putter down from the sky and felt the displaced air as it landed near me.

"You're done early, bro!" I heard him laugh, but he must have noticed that I was crouching in the dark parking lot, holding my head. "Oh damn, bro, you used protection, right? Dad'll kill me!"

INTERLUDE

Well, that one was stupid. An e-STD from sex with a robot? I don't want to think too hard about the logistics of that one and suggest you do the same.

You're still here! I really am thrilled!

A few thoughts on writing…

It's really cool. I like doing it.

A few more thoughts…

Years ago, I was on the phone with my mom. I lived in Livonia, MI and she was in Columbus, OH; more than a three-hour drive apart. She asked, "have you seen the moon tonight?" and I walked out on my back deck to check it out a stunning, full moon. I voiced some thoughts about how magical it is that we're two hundred miles apart, talking instantly using technology neither of us understood, looking at the same object almost two hundred and forty thousand miles away.

Writing is, in a way, very similar.

I'm putting these words down at 10:30pm on June 13, 2022 and when are you reading them? You and I are separated by time and distance. I hope

I'm still alive when you read this, but maybe I died a hundred years ago, and this is part of your required reading for texts from before The Fall. From back when polar bears and tigers existed, though only barely. Will you have to translate the date I gave at the start of the paragraph to the calendar system now in use? Maybe the screen reader will do that automatically.

Flat text lacks the inflection and other cues of spoken language, but I'm writing fiction here. Most of what I type out will play in your head differently than it did in mine. My goal is usually to get your image as close to mine, in so far as it actually matters. What does Senior Detective McClacky sound like? Have you met him yet? You will. He's two weeks from retirement, but he gets around. How did you pronounce a name like Ronxif? Or were they just N and R in that story?

The point is, writing is an amazing tool for asynchronous communication. I write something now and you read it in a month or a century. Or I read it a century from now because my consciousness has been uploaded. Or I read it in a week and completely forgot that I put all this down tonight. I am very sleepy...

ROBOPEDE

Without looking, I reached for my pen, but it wasn't where I last dropped it on my desk. I glanced over and recoiled in disgust at the centipede coiled around my gel pen. Beside it, scrawled in sloppy, shaky handwriting, was a note. "Help me! I've been turned into a centipede!" it said.

I shifted my suspicious glare between the note and the bug. "Did you write this?"

The centipede struggled with the pen and managed a messy "Y" on the paper.

"And what were you before you were turned into a centipede?"

M...A...N

I stared at the letters for a long moment. "If you say so. How were you turned into a centipede? A witch? Ancient curse?"

D...O...N...T...K...N...O...W

"Well, I don't know how you expect me to help you, if you can't supply even the smallest bit of context."

It tapped the word "Help" at the top of the note.

I crossed my arms and leaned into the back of my chair. "What if a witch did this to you and said whomever lends assistance will share a similar fate? Would you do that to me? A total stranger?"

N...O...T...S...

I turned away for my last sip of tea while it wrote.

T...R...A...N...G...E...R

"Not a stranger? You're saying I knew you pre-centipede?"

It tapped the Y and kept writing.

"You know, you should have just written the whole alphabet out once and we could have Ouija boarded this."

M...I...K...E

"Mike? From accounting?" I brought my eyes close and squinted at its bug face. It twitched its mandibles at me. "I know how it sounds, since you're a bug, but you don't look like how Mike from accounting would look as a centipede."

M...A...I...L...R

"Oh Mailroom Mike, yeah, yeah, I see that now. Say, I was having the DVD box set of Frasier sent to the office, since I don't trust deliveries sitting outside my apartment. Did you see that down there, by chance? Before..." I waved at him.

The bug tapped "Help" again.

"No point in getting testy, Mike," I sighed. "I'm still not convinced of what's going on here. Tell me something only a human, and not a natural centipede, would know."

It paused for a long moment and I thought I had tricked it.

3...1...4...1...5...2...

"Ah! Wrong! But I guess that proves something. I assume centipedes wouldn't know mathematical constants, and you knew pi to four digits." I got close to the bug again. "That doesn't prove you're not a robot centipede controlled by advanced AI sent here to assess the gullibility of humans. Can you compose a sonnet about the nature of love?"

The centipede froze a moment before circling the letters "NO".

"Yeah, that might not be a fair one. I don't think I could write a sonnet. I'm not really sure what a sonnet is. Last chance, robo-bug. Tell me, how come time flies like an arrow, but fruit flies like a banana?"

?...?

"Ha! I knew it! Some advanced AI you are!" I wrestled my pen from the centipede AI masquerading as Mailroom Mike and covered it with my empty tea mug. I glanced at the clock: 4:57 on Friday. This was a Monday problem to solve.

MADAM ZERZONI, HR

"That has to be a typo," said Sean beside me, along with a wave of black coffee and nicotine on his breath.

"Typo? It's a single number written in dry-erase," I said and chewed my cheek.

"Typo, write-o, you know what I mean."

"Why would someone write a negative number?" I took a sip from my thermos. "Someone in the office just updates the days since..." I waved at Sean's cane.

"I bet it's that new woman in HR. The one with the scarves and jingly jewelry." He coughed into the back of his hand.

Our section chief brought Madam Zerzoni through last week during her orientation. Despite her flowing indigo dress and jangling belt of bells, I'd quickly forgotten about her as she disappeared behind the office doors overlooking the factory. A chill ran across my arms now as I recalled the way she gripped my hand with fingers like ice and stared at me with a gaze that pierced my soul. I thought the long night kept awake by the baying of wild dogs and vivid terrors had been because of the taco cart I stopped at for dinner.

I glanced up at the office windows and caught a glint of silver bells as the horizontal blinds snapped shut.

"Whelp, I gotta get back to it," Sean huffed.

I watched my older coworker return to his station, shuffling on a leg that refused to heal quite right.

I finished the tomato soup in my thermos and went back to my station. The number taunted me when I passed the sign outside the break room twice more that afternoon to hit the john and again on my way out after the shift whistle blew.

Why a negative number? Did that mean something would happen tomorrow? No one could know that, unless an accident was planned... but then it wouldn't be an accident. The sign said "Days since workplace incident", nothing about an *accident...*

"Have a pleasant evening, Mr. Senin."

The smoky voice snapped me from the reverie as I walked out the door to the car park.

I gasped and hopped away. I coughed to clear my throat. "Madam Zerzoni, hello there."

She stood just fifteen feet from the door,

wearing a royal purple dress that hugged her slender frame and pooled around her feet. A half dozen thin chain belts wrapped around her waist, jiggling bells as she took a step toward me.

"Please," she started, and brought the long cigarette holder to her lips for a deep inhale. She blew the smoke to the ceiling. "Call me Madam Zerzoni."

"I…" I was pretty sure that was exactly what I'd called her, but I felt less certain as she stared at me, unblinking. Her eyes, hazel with striations of something darker, latched onto my gaze until I managed a sharp sniff and looked away. "Have a nice evening."

I turned toward the door to the stairs.

"Pleasant evening to you, Mr. Senin. Take care driving," she called out as I put my hand on the door. "Avoid University Street tonight, and I hope to see you tomorrow."

I looked back at her whispered warning, but only a trail of smoke hung in the air where she had stood.

Rushing up two flights, my keys fumbled at the lock until I finally got into my car. Taking gulps of air that reeked of car wash pine and stale french fries, my knuckles blanched white on the steering wheel as I tried to slow my breathing. Sean had to be right; the negative number on the incident board was a warning of imminent danger in the factory. Part of me immediately agreed with him, that it was Madam Zerzoni's doing, but why? Because she wears four scarves at once in June? No, this was some weird metaphysical worry with no basis in reality. No one can predict the future. No one could know something would happen tomorrow. Not unless they planned it.

My heart at last settled back into my chest and I spiraled down the ramp and onto Ninth Avenue. I stopped at the red lights and paused at the yields, completely on autopilot, until I looked up from the blinking flash of my right-turn signal. The line of cars in front of me waiting to turn onto University Street was longer than normal.

University Street.

I yanked the wheel left and cut off a rusted pickup truck in my hurry to heed Madam Zerzoni's cryptic warning. The drone of a horn and shouted curses faded as I cut across the street. A block later, I saw the Decent-Mart sign and pulled in, remembering I'd drank the last of my milk with breakfast. The traffic in the street, all waiting to turn onto University Street from the other direction, stretched another block. I stepped from my car and chuckled at the distant sound of jackhammers. Construction, that's all Madam Zerzoni was warning me about. Not that she was prophesying some terrible car accident, but warning me to avoid summer construction.

My cheeks and neck flushed with embarrassment for a thing I alone shared in as I stepped past the whooshing automatic doors into the brisk chill of the Decent-Mart. They always kept this place too cold, even in the winter. I grabbed a cart and found some mild comfort in the simple act of wending my way through the aisles, picking out food stuffs without a thought about how they might combine into a meal.

My last stop was the dairy cooler. I dug to the back, finding the gallon with the latest date as the frigid mist flowed around my shoulders.

"Hello, Mr. Senin."

I jerked from the cooler and caught the gallon of milk that nearly slipped from my fingers.

Frozen mist pooled around the hem of Madam Zerzoni's dress and she pulled her shawls a little. How did she get here so fast?

"I see you took my advice," she said and carefully placed a half-gallon of Deer Trax in her cart.

I chuckled again. "Yes, thank you. I forgot the construction was starting this week." I stole a glance over at what else she'd gathered from the store. Three bunches of bananas, bags of flour or sugar, bulk oil, no fewer than eight bottles of red wine. Maybe she was planning to make banana bread and drink while doing it. Seeing the average purchases dispelled some of the mysticism about her.

When I looked away from her cart, she stood within arm's reach of me, staring up at me with those piercing eyes. I yelped and jumped back.

"Avoid your usuals, or you won't make it to work tomorrow, Mr. Senin."

My eyes blurred with the burn of smoke, and when I blinked it away, she was gone. Her new warning or threat echoed in my ears while I quickly debated abandoning my cart to rush back to my apartment. I took a deep breath and forced myself to wait in line to pay.

Groceries in hand, my shoulders did a little happy dance as I passed the taco stand on the way to my front door. Alberto parked his cart there every Tuesday and every tenant of my building waited in line for his walking taco specialty. Last week's left me with cramps that I was now certain had nothing to do with meeting Madam Zerzoni earlier in the day. Despite that, I had every intention of putting the groceries away, changing from my factory uniform, and being down here to wait in line within a half hour.

Though... Was this my usual habit that Madam Zerzoni warned about? As much as it would have been nice for her to be more explicit in her warning, she was right about avoiding University Street. Maybe I should avoid a taco and eat a microwaved turkey hot dog instead.

No, that's stupid. She remembered the construction on University. The factory didn't hire a damn psychic for HR.

I repeated that to myself while the microwave beeped and I took out my turkey dog. NBC-3 was showing an all-night marathon of *Law and Order: Double Jeopardy* and I settled into that, not even bothering to shower off the glitter from the day's work. Grabbing my phone, I texted Sean about the marathon. He loved this show.

I woke myself with a snore. The TV showed only static and by the darkness out my window, I must have been out for hours. I clicked off the TV and was hit by the total silence. Eerie quiet that pressed on my eardrums. Looking back at the window, I saw a single snowflake drift across the pane, then another.

Snow in June?

I stood and crossed to the window overlooking

the street four stories down. A fine layer of snow covered the parked cars.

Not snow.

Ash.

Bodies lay still between the cars.

I snorted awake as some kid screamed outside my window. A scream of joy. It probably had sparklers or those stupid things that pop when you throw them at the ground. The sun was still up, though barely, and another episode of *Double Jeopardy* was starting as the credits for the previous episode whizzed by. I hauled myself up and shook off the lingering intensity of the nightmare. Eveningmare?

Knowing I'd get no sleep, I brushed my teeth, undressed, and slid into bed. Checking my phone, no response from Sean. That was weird. I picked up the half-finished James Patterson on my nightstand, hoping something with bad pacing and poor editing would put me out. Four hours later, the sun had set, and I finished the last page without my eyelids feeling any heavier.

I heaved a sigh and smelled a hint of distant cigarette smoke. Stupid brain playing tricks on me. I got up and played Minecraft naked in my living room until my phone alarm went off. It was time to get up, or at least time to decide if I would go to work. Other than my brief eveningmare, I hadn't slept. That was a valid reason to call off.

My mind ticked through the arguments of how sick time is a right and by not taking it, I was cutting into my wages. I whispered and grumbled the impassioned debate even while I showered and put on a clean uniform. I avoided University Street while eating a cold Pop Tart and looped up to my regular spot. Passing the same cars I did every day, carrying my thermoses of soup and coffee, I paused for only a half step at the number zero written with a flourished loop before entering the break room. By the silence broken only by the slurp of coffee and occasional cough, I knew the others on my shift were as nervous as I. The analog log clock read 6:58. There was still time for me to slip out and cite a sudden stomach bug.

Where was Sean? He'd never been late for a shift.

The clap of hard leather on tile turned everyone's attention to the door. My section chief stood between Madam Zerzoni and Sean. My coworker looked awkward in a button-up and tie.

The shift whistle blew.

"I hope you don't mind me taking a moment at the start of shift," said my section chief. "Ogrora Farms Corporate loves nothing more than to promote from within the organization. You've all met Madam Zerzoni, who just transferred from the East Leon packaging plant and she suggested a most interesting exercise. Our workplace can be dangerous if not for the careful eye of our skilled workforce." She paused to gesture to the group of us in the break room. "But it's not always enough to notice, but also to report what we see. I'm sure many of your noticed the change to the incident board yesterday, but only Mr. Duskridge," she waved at Sean, "came to me to inquire. I offered, and he has accepted a position at the East Leon junior management track."

The group chattered their approval and mild cheers. The room slowly emptied as each stopped to congratulate Sean and shake his hand.

A stupid corporate test, that's all it was. Whoever reported something strange in the workplace would get a promotion. I hung around and watched the crowd thin, taking a slow sip from my coffee thermos.

"Mr. Senin," said a smoky voice at my left.

I choked and coughed on the coffee. Madam Zerzoni was beside Sean when I lifted my thermos... how did she move so fast?

"Madam Zerzoni." I swallowed and coughed once more. "I have to say, this stunt had me a nervous wreck. I thought something bad was going to happen today, as if someone could see the future." My nervous chuckle faded with the seriousness in her eyes. "Um, what did you mean last night in the mart about me avoiding my usuals? I didn't get the tacos I always do on Tuesday because of what you said."

"Think of the sodium, fat, and cholesterol you avoided, Mr. Senin," she said with the ghost of a grin.

"You said I wouldn't make it into work if I didn't?"

"Mr. Duskridge will perform well in East Leon," she said, glancing at Sean by the door, "but you were my first pick. If only you had seized the opportunities I gave you, Mr. Senin. Good day to you."

She glided past Sean and from the room, leaving me alone with a thermos of coffee halfway to my lips.

VANILLA, PUMPKIN SPICE, DEATH

Senior Detective McClacky flicked his cigarette to the curb and ducked under the yellow tape.

"What do we got?" he asked the officer that couldn't have been older than fourteen.

"Victim is Mina Zeoli, 27. First on the scene responded to a 9-1-1 at 4:17am. Neighbor said it sounded like the victim was," he consulted the pad in his hand, "screaming loud enough to wake the dead."

McClacky popped an antacid and pulled heavily on the handrail up to the second floor. Two weeks from retirement, why couldn't the chief put someone else on this? Forensics snapped pictures inside an apartment littered with little yellow, numbered markers. McClacky's fingers traced over the damaged doorjamb as he stepped in among them.

"The door and windows were all locked," said the baby officer. "Officers had to force entry."

Before the events of last night, this cute little one-bedroom walkup probably smelled of vanilla and pumpkin spice. Sitting near the door, a yoga mat and blocks poked from a canvas bag with "#NAMASTEBITCHES" printed in bold, looping letters. A dozen succulents in clear glass terrariums hung by the sliding door to the balcony. A black and white print of Audrey Hepburn filled the wall over a cream-colored loveseat covered in a chunky knitted throw. McClacky rolled his eyes and sighed at the "Live Laugh Love" stencil over a rack of cheap white wines.

He stepped around it all and whistled when he saw into the bedroom. Forensics would take fewer pictures here if they only photographed places *not* dripping in blood. A single set of boot prints led to and from the bed, but the coroner's journey had been nothing but a formality. She could have confirmed the deceased status of the victim from the doorway by the mangled twist of her limbs.

"The coroner wanted you on the scene before she released the body," said the infant. "She said she's never seen anything like this and had to go outside. What in God's name could do something like this? She... She's inside out."

"God?" McClacky turned and fumbled another tablet from his pocket. "God has nothing to do with this. Keep the press away while we look for a boyfriend and all that shit, but this makes three.

We've got a serial killer on our hands."

He popped two more antacids.

Two weeks from retirement.

* * *

"Cause of death is…" Maggie MacAtilla waved her arms over the lumps of flesh and organs. "There's really no way tae know if she was dead 'fore havin' her insides on tha outside."

McClacky handed the county's chief medical examiner a fresh coffee before taking a sip from his own. "Is there anything that might cause this?"

"Nothing natural. You said there was two more?"

McClacky nodded. "One from upstate two days ago, and another the day before by the coast. Locals are keeping it all hush-hush because, well, obviously. Can't have the press knowing young girls are imploding."

"Invertin's more like it."

McClacky grimaced and shook his head. "I'll get the files from the other cases and send you what I can."

* * *

Thanks to the department's diligent administrator, two thick folders wrapped in rubber bands awaited him on his desk. He sat and opened the first one, leafing through pages of coroner and field reports, credit card and phone details, and statements from neighbors.

The three victims were of similar age and went to the same university upstate four years ago. Both files before him showed credit card purchases on the same date and time last Friday evening at the same deli in a town two hours west of here. When the admin placed the folder containing Mina Zeoli's details in front of him with a charge at that same deli, the picture in McClacky's mind snapped into focus.

"I found something that might be useful," said Wallace O'Shane, the junior detective that sat across from McClacky. The red-bearded buck stepped around the desk to show his phone to McClacky, scrolling through a gallery of young women in tight t-shirts and short shorts. "It's Mina's InstaFeed profile. Check out her last post."

McClacky lifted his reading glasses to see the screen. "Wine weekend with my ladies! #wine #winelover #besties #vino #wineoclock #aurora" The picture showed four women holding oversized glasses of red wine in front of an electric fireplace.

McClacky recognized the other two victims.

"Who's the fourth girl?" He pointed to the one on the right, a platinum blonde with high cheekbones wearing an oversized sweatshirt from the same upstate university.

O'Shane scrolled through the post and tapped a few links. "Jessica Reds," he said, and kept tapping. "She has an address in town."

McClacky already had his coat in hand. "Let's roll."

* * *

No response at the door. McClacky circled the bungalow, cupping his hands over his eyes to peek in windows, while O'Shane went the other direction. They met at the backdoor.

"Nothing," said the junior detective, and McClacky banged on the door. Still no response.

"Call it in." McClacky took a handkerchief from his pocket, wrapped it around his fist, and smashed through the thin plate-glass window in the door. He reached through to flip the lock. "Police," he announced. "Jessica Reds, are you home?"

O'Shane finished with dispatch and tucked his phone away to follow the older detective with a flashlight in hand. The kitchen held the charm one might expect from a person thrice Reds' age with light wood paneling, lace curtains, and a bowl of fake fruit on the formica countertop.

Something thumped on the floor above them.

They passed quickly through to the living room and turned to the stairs by the front door leading to the second level.

"Police! We're coming up," McClacky called and put a hand over his sidearm, thumbing off the snap. He moved quickly, but with seasoned caution. The bathroom at the top of the steps looked empty at a quick glance, but the dark bedroom on the right was a duplicate of what McClacky saw only hours before.

The detectives rushed in with flashlights and guns drawn, trying not to focus on the horror on the bed. Their beams swept across the room and caught the movement of something too small to be a person. A dog or animal? It was gone faster than either man could focus on it. They searched under the bed and in the open closet.

"Must have been a trick of our lights," said McClacky, not convincing even himself.

Sirens blared outside and O'Shane rushed to unlock the door. Alone in the room, McClacky focused his light on the bed with a frown. Two weeks from retirement, he couldn't leave this case unsolved. He lowered his flashlight beam with a deep sigh, noting the strong vanilla and pumpkin spice scent. The light settled on a business card laying on the carpet's thick shag. He bent to pick it up. "Aurora Cabin, available for rent, call or email…" He flipped it over. "3/12-3/14" was printed in looping handwriting. Last weekend.

Over thirty years on the force, McClacky learned good police work was as much about following a hunch as it was following protocol. He pocketed the card. He stepped into the bathroom to let the medical staff pass before quietly leaving the bungalow.

* * *

The headlights of his old Chevette illuminated the cabin's front porch. McClacky stubbed out his third cigarette and pulled the flask from his jacket's inner pocket. Something about the drive through the woods and the crooked smirk of the weird man at the gas station set him on edge. A bit of grandma's medicine would help calm him. He breathed out the cheap bourbon's sharp bite and felt it warm its way to his belly.

McClacky turned off the engine and punched

the code into the lockbox fixed to the front door. Key in hand, he entered the cabin. Fumbling for the light switch, the smell of vanilla and pumpkin spice overwhelmed him.

Something flittered through the shadows at the corner of his vision.

ROLL TO HIT

Tankcat kept his eyes focused straight ahead and his jacket clenched tight at his throat. This part of town came with a hundred terrible rumors and if anyone one of them were right, he would be lucky to make it back home in one piece.

A woman some years past her prime, wearing a skirt and tube top far too small, strolled to intersect his path. "Where you goin' in such a hurry, sweet thang?"

"No thank you, ma'am," he muttered and stepped around her.

"You lookin' to buy some Gygax? I got all the editions here," called a man from the shadows and Tankcat hastened his pace. The tiny map display in the bottom-right of his field of vision showed he was almost there.

The sound of deep bass came at the edge of his hearing, providing a beat to the constant, distant police sirens. Tankcat turned the last corner and looked up to "Beholder's Den" blaring from the hologram across the storefront, mimicking the look of an ancient neon sign. He hurried to descend the half flight of steps and looked up at the bouncer, a hulking gorilla of a man, standing sentinel beside the door. Tankcat fumbled with his jacket and extended a hand. His state ID, lightly forged, appeared in the space over his palm, but the bouncer waved him by without taking a closer look.

Pushing the door open, the den's interior closed around him; something out of an old holographic of what people thought the future might look like. Synthogirls danced around poles on small, elevated stages while old men sat around watching them impotently. Small, private booths dominated the back and left side of the den, and only a quarter of them were occupied. Along the right side, a long bar dominated the wall, covered with colorful liquor bottles from a dozen worlds. The bartender, another synth, slid along his track to serve and clean.

Tankcat kept his head down and hood up as he made for the closest unoccupied booth. Within his jacket, one hand touched the leatherette pouch while he tried his best to look natural and relaxed as he slid into the seat. It wasn't too late. He could still get up and leave, forget this whole venture. He would be home before his aunt even noticed.

Minutes ticked by, or maybe just seconds, and he could feel his nerves fraying, his resolve weakening. He scooted to the edge of the booth just as someone flopped onto the cushion opposite him.

"You weren't leaving, were you?" said the gravelly voice he recognized from the voicechat, going by the handle Atomicoid. They pushed back their hood to reveal a man's face of maybe thirty hard summers. An implant whirred from his left eye.

Tankcat settled back but did not relax. "No, I just was going to get a drink."

Atomicoid snapped his fingers, and a waitress was at the table a breath later.

"What are you drinking?" she said in her synthesized voice.

"Two D6s and..." Atomicoid looked at Tankcat with a devilish grin. "And two vials of Gygax. I like to wet my whistle before doing business."

"Sure thang," said the waitress and zipped away.

Tankcat's heart pounded in his ears. Was it too late to bail? "I have other clients to get to tonight," Tankcat lied. "Maybe we can just do this and be on our ways?" He tried not to stare at Atomicoid's fake eye. It was an older style replacement with most of the machinery exposed.

Atomicoid leaned back and crossed his arms. "Let me see your face. I want to see who I'm dealing with."

Tankcat reached with sweaty palms to push back the hood of his jacket, feeling suddenly naked and exposed in the harsh light of the bar.

Atomicoid whistled. "You either got access to some great quality serum, or you're just a kid. That you're meeting in this shithole, I'm guessing the second."

The waitress returned and set a squat glass of bubbling, orange liquid in front of them each, then a thin vial beside those. Tankcat couldn't stop his curiosity as he leaned closed to note how the vial balanced on a sharp conical base.

"You ever done Gygax before?" Atomicoid flicked the vial in front of him to make it spin like a top.

Tankcat considered lying but worried it might spiral into a worse predicament. "No."

Atomicoid reached across the table to take the drink in front of Tankcat and gestured to the vial. "You keep that as a gift, kid. There's nothing like it, exploring whole worlds in your mind." He grinned and downed the bubbling drink. "Let me see what you got."

Tankcat froze for a breath before remembering the pouch in his jacket. He took it out and passed it across the table. Atomicoid pushed it off the edge beside him and nodded with the thump of bass when he looked inside. "I'll trust I won't have to count it. I'll come get the rest from you if anything's missing." He took a similar bag from his coat and slid it to Tankcat, who slipped it into his jacket without looking inside.

"Thanks," he said and scooted out of the booth.

"Hey, kid."

Tankcat clutched his coat tight and looked back at Atomicoid. He held out the vial of Gygax, playfully rolling it between two fingers. Tankcat snatched the vial and fled the bar, leaving its syntholadies and illegal drugs behind.

He walked as quickly as he could without looking frightened. The fear of getting caught overtook him and he jogged, and finally sprinted, always following the map in the bottom-right of his vision. He only stopped to fall against a brick wall when the sirens were barely audible.

He dared a peek and pulled out the pouch, loosening the nylon strings. A dozen gems glimmered back at him in the low light. Two of each type of cut with four, six, eight, ten, twelve, or twenty sides each. Tankcat plucked a twenty-sided die from the bag and rolled the nearly spherical gem between his thumb and forefinger, feeling the sharp edges poke at his fingerprints.

Carefully placing the vial of Gygax beside the gems, Tankcat ran the rest of the way back to his aunt's apartment.

* * *

If you were unsure of the references in this story, ask your nerd friends about the history of Dungeons and Dragons and how it was perceived early on, or Google "d&d satanic panic".

THE GRIND

The bell jingled, signaling the end of Stord's break. He pushed from his wobbly chair with a groan and wiped the grease from his hands on his ripped trousers. Taking up his rusted short sword, he trudged from the staff room and down the long hall to the spawn room. He grumbled when Utak stepped beside him.

"Another day, another loot token, eh, Stord?" said the chatty ogre.

Stord looked up at the hunched, warty creature carrying a small tree trunk as a club and grinned a gap-toothed smile, but said nothing. He learned the hard way that engaging with Utak only made the ogre talk until Stord wished for the sweet release of an adventurer's hammer through his skull.

Stord waved for Utak to go ahead as the mass funneled into a single line. The ogre punched his card and received his assignment for the day.

"Mid boss in the treasury!" he shouted back. "Maybe I'll see you there!"

Utak stepped into the center of the stone dais

and disappeared.

Stord took his timecard and stamped it as he had every day for the last three thousand and eighteen spawn cycles. The overseer handed him a card with his duty, "Treasury trash mob." He cursed to himself, but smiled at the overseer. He learned a long time ago that requesting a change only leads to punishing and/or a week without pay.

As he mounted the dais, he tried to remember what series of misfortunes brought him to this point. His parents always raved about what a bright goblin he was and how he was destined for great things. He may even be the first goblin president! Most days working in The Underlord's Dungeon came and went with little trouble. Sometimes he would help to kill a hero, some of those times he would even be the one to land the killing blow. More often than not, the day would end with an arrow in his face or a sword in his face or a firebolt in his face. Despite being called "heroes", they really enjoyed killing him in the face. No matter the outcome, the pay was the same and with his tenure, he did well enough. There were certainly worse ways for a goblin to make a living.

Now he was about to spend a full day beside

Utak the Ogre and his incessant banter boring into his mind.

The cold, stone walls disappeared and were replaced with a sea of gold coins, crowns, treasure boxes, and embellished swords. They assigned Stord here often enough, and he knew the room was mostly worthless decoration and the only thing of value would be in the chest behind the mid-boss. His goblin mind still salivated over the display of wealth.

"Stord!" Utak bellowed from where he stood beside a throne made of pure gold. "You're going to protect me today! I'm so happy! We're halfway through the dungeon, so there's time for me to tell you about that foot surgery I just had. I know you were wondering why I've been out for a week."

Stord looked around at his two dozen fellow goblins and two kobolds and wondered if he could get lost amongst them. They all hefted short swords like Stord had or short bows and the kobolds each had a withered staff.

Utak plopped on the throne and lifted his right foot to his lap. "So they had to cut in here too—"

A gentle chime turned all eyes to the main door into the treasure room. A light above it flashed yellow, signaling the heroes were in the room before.

J. M. Samland

"Already?" Utak frowned and stood, picking up his tree club. "Archers in back, casters by me, swords in front."

The goblins and kobolds barely made it into position before the door slid open and mist flowed through. The trash mobs and mid-boss looked around in confusion for only a moment before the nearest exploded in a spray of blood.

Assassin rogue, Stord thought with a groan. The dungeon saw more of these in the last week and they were a nightmare to kill so long as they remained stealthed. Why they remained stealthed after an attack was a question Stord kept meaning to ask his manager. Merely as a question of understanding, not a complaint.

The kobolds on either side of Utak waved their magic staves, and the room filled with an icy mist. Stord couldn't guess the reason until another two goblins exploded and a pair of boot tracks became clear in the snow coating the mounds of coins. The other goblins saw it and swung their swords. Another fell to the assassin before the killer took a solid blow and their stealth dropped.

A female human, if Stord correctly remembered from his class in monster races, stood among the goblins for a long breath, a long dagger in one hand and holding her bleeding shoulder with the

82

other. Stord tightened his grip on his sword. There was no monetary gain for killing the hero, but her death would mean he could go home early.

Steel whirled. For every two goblins the assassin felled, she took another slash. Utak cheered them on from beside his throne. Stord waited for his chance to strike, stepping closer with each of his kind the rogue took down. Glee swelled in Stord's chest, noticing how the assassin ran out of tricks and chugged her last healing potion. Only a few goblins remained, and Stord stepped forward for his turn.

"Wait!" the human shouted, and despite the thrill of battle, Stord, the other trash mobs, and Utak fell silent and still. "An offer! I'm recruiting for a new dungeon. One with a fairer overseer, better pay and working conditions. Lead me from here and you may join me."

Beady goblin eyes stared at her. Kobold snouts twitched.

"Medical?" asked a goblin on the other side of the assassin.

The rogue nodded. "And dental."

The goblin grinned, exposing a row of gapped, crooked teeth.

Other goblins lowered their weapons, but Stord's experience kept his suspicion high. The assassin class was notorious for its tricks, but offering to employ a room full of monsters was one he'd never heard before. Still, what if she was being truthful and her offer real? Stord thought of his one-bedroom apartment with one hundred and sixteen square feet of luxury and a shared bathroom down the hall. Located on the seventeenth sublevel only nine blocks from the train station, what more could he really want from life?

Half the remaining goblins dropped their weapon, as well as both kobolds and Utak. Stord felt the tip of his own blade lower.

* * *

"And then what happened?" asked the small, green goblin with wide, beady eyes.

"We helped the assassin clear the dungeon, and she held true to her promise. I left The Underlord's Dungeon and started work at The Forsaken Crypts. That's where I met your grandnan."

"And you became rich? Why aren't you president?"

Stord laughed and patted the child on her head. "We do well enough. We bought this hovel together." Stord gestured to the three-room hut around him. "No one gets rich working for someone else, and we're too old now to start our own dungeon."

"When I grow up, I want to own the largest, most deadliest dungeon ever!"

Stord grinned, exposing a row of straight, white teeth, and patted his granddaughter on the head again. "I'm sure you will, Teaks. I'm sure all the mightiest heroes will meet their end by the beasts you employ."

The girl's grin widened as she giggled.

Thus began the tale of Underlord Teaks the Unbearable, Scourge of the Kingsland, Devourer of Nations, Breaker of Souls.

LEGACY

Time for me to yammer again for a minute!

Most of these stories started from writing prompts. You've probably already heard that from the book blurb or the intro or personally from me as I was pressuring you to buy the book. There are a number that didn't make the cut.

The princess lives with the demon prince. She wants to help the demon prince with his dungeon design when she learns her father sent her here to use the demon prince as bait to find the right knight to marry her. The demon prince is also wildly flamboyant.

The princess — a different princess, lots of princesses in this thing — is left alone while the king takes the army to fight. Then she has to defend the city when a greater army attacks. Of course, the "greater army" is the king coming back as undead.

The hero risks everything to acquire the legendary sword. Turns out it's a piece of crap; worthless in combat, but its reputation will sway a battle. I set that one in Kamakura Period Japan and was a lot of fun to research. Also horrifying.

Nappa from Dragonball Z and Jaskier from The Witcher go on a date. That was a lot of fun to write a seven-foot-tall Saiyan warrior being the sub for a scrawny bard with a heron feather hat, but just sounds like a big ball of copyright infringement to publish.

A couple of inept dryads summon the Lich Lord to kill and enslave the humans invading their forest. That's probably the general plot of a dozen direct-to-video cartoons from the 90s.

"So Jamie," you ask. "With so much garbage to pick from, how do you decide what gems go into this tome?"

So kind of you to ask.

I'll pivot back to another story about my mother. I'm the second born and, were my sister a boy, my parents would have named her Jeremy. So I asked mom once, "Why wasn't I Jeremy?" She said the name just didn't fit anymore. At least I think she said something like that... I'll make myself a note to confirm that story before you read this.

Like the scenes in a novel, some things just won't make the cut. Maybe they didn't pan out like I envisioned or didn't express the theme I'd hoped they would. Maybe they got clumsy or rambled. Or… What is this chapter called?

Legacy.

Oh yeah, that.

To spoil a little of *Trials of Throk'tar*, Daelin wants his son to have kids. Though he doesn't say it directly — and not saying things directly is his major problem — it's because he's proud of his own children. There's a drive to leave something behind when you're gone. That might be a slab of limestone with your name and couple of dates, shaping the minds of kindergarteners for forty years, creating some piece of art, raising your own children and subsequent generations, getting angry with the natural progress as the world leaves you behind.

What was my point? Let's get back to the stories. Something with robots. At least one robot.

PLEASANT DAY, CHARLIE JACOBSON

"Pardon me, sir. Do you have the time?"

Charlie turned at the synthesized voice and ran his gaze over the six-foot-tall robot. His focus landed on the jagged, pulsing antenna coming from its head, before glancing around at the foot traffic passing them without a care.

"You're a robot," Charlie stated the obvious.

"I am. Do you have the time, sir?"

Charlie glanced at his watch. "12:34. Don't you have an internal chronometer to tell you that?"

"Thank you, sir. It was damaged in my transfer here."

Charlie blinked at the sunlight gleaming off the robot's steel chassis and wondered why no one else seemed to notice or care as they strode by. "Well... good day." He turned from the robot, toward the direction of his office. He noticed the robot beside him a few steps later.

"It seems we are going the same way, sir," it said.

"So it seems." Charlie straightened the knot of

his tie and coughed. "Robots must be pretty common in New York City, huh?"

"I should think not, sir."

"Really?" Charlie glanced at the men and women passing in their business casual, noticing how no one acknowledged or cared about the tin person. "You'd really stand out in my hometown in Kentucky."

"Go Wildcats!" the robot exclaimed and pumped a segmented fist into the air.

They continued in silence for another moment, surrounded by the constant blare of horns from annoyed taxi drivers and the whir of gears and clomp of heavy steps from the robot. Charlie turned left toward his law office and the robot remained by his side.

"It appears we are still going the same way, sir," it said. "My probability circuits balk at the chance we are going to the same location in a human city this size."

"Human city? How large are robot cities compared to New York?"

"Robot cities," it said with a chord of notes like a laugh. "Why would robots need cities?"

"I..." Charlie stammered. "I guess for all the robot delis and robot dentists and robot law firms."

It laughed again. "I believe the human adage is

to imply you watch too much science fiction, Charlie Jacobson."

"How do you know my name?" Charlie looked down at his briefcase, sure nothing more than his initials were engraved by the metal clasp.

He looked back up at the robot and gasped. The blare of horns faded to silence as the world slowed to total stillness.

"I like you, Charlie Jacobson. You gave me the time, and you made me laugh. You will be spared. Pleasant day."

Sound and movement exploded around Charlie as time resumed its normal flow. People were running and screaming, pointing to the sky. Charlie looked up at the craft as large as five city blocks obscuring the noon sun. A score of portals opened along its bottom like the iris of a camera lens and belched a swarm of beasts with long, serpentine bodies and leathery wings.

The swarm of dragons descended upon New York City.

NO, YOU GET MURDERED FIRST!

The park ranger wears a big, stupid hat and tells the group how to identify poison ivy. At least, I think she is. I watched *Mamma Mia* during the ferry ride and *Gimme! Gimme! Gimme!* is playing on loop in my head. Just the chorus, naturally. God… Meryl Streep is a national treasure.

"…Hang your food from the trees or the micro bears will…"

Won't somebody help me chase the shadows away?

"…If you have an emergency, you can return to the dock…"

Take me through the darkness to the break of the day.

"Any other questions?" The ranger locks eyes with me for a breath before she grins across the young couples and two larger groups, nineteen in total, then leads the few that were interested to point out what poison ivy looks like. I heft my pack and stride past them all, remembering each of their faces, nearly giddy wondering who would be my special friend tonight.

"You are now entering the wilderness," reads

the sign and I follow the crude path another kilometer into the woods before cutting a hundred meters into the undergrowth. My camo tent only takes a few minutes to set up and I nestle inside to pull off my boots.

I set the alarm on my phone for 2:45am and hear the group of seven over on the path. One man makes comments about how beautiful it all is, while another suggests they go to the shipwreck overlook tomorrow. One first-time island camper, one veteran.

Both last time island campers.

I hum a random ABBA chorus while I lay the contents of my pack out in an array before me on my sleeping bag. Two large knives, three small, a hand crossbow with eight bolts, blow dart gun, garrot wire, flashlight, nitrile gloves, and a plastic portable urinal. The gloves aren't really necessary, but they were on sale and it's not like they took up any space or weight. My fingers trace along the most worn of the knives. As much as I took care of my tools, this one saw the most use. More than a few times, I thought to name the blade with the gaudy red grip, but that's something crazy people do. I secure all the tools on the leather harness I'll wear tonight before tucking into my sleeping bag. The day may be young, but I have over twenty square kilometers to scour tonight. I need my beauty sleep.

Taking one last item from my bag, I lay the square, maroon envelope on my chest and cover it with both hands.

I focus on the drone of insects and drift off to the stillness of the warm afternoon.

Birdsong wakes me.

"Shit shit shit!"

I grab for a phone that isn't there. Panic seizes me when I see the leather harness with my tools disturbed and it doesn't take more than a cursory glance to notice the red handle is gone. This wasn't micro bears getting into my tent. I think through the nineteen at orientation. One of them must have recognized me. But as I recall each face, none had shown any lasting interest. Only the park ranger made eye contact with me.

Unless...

Breaking the black wax seal with the rose stamp on the red envelope, my trembling fingers unfold the single sheet and the three words are exactly what I expect and what I least hope for.

The Park Ranger.

I curse her and her big, stupid hat as I unzip the tent and poke my head out. Through the dense canopy, a sky slowly wakes with streaks of blue, putting the time at just after 5am. The one person who knows the island better than I has a two and half hour lead. Stealing the competition's phone and tools may not be against the letter of the rules of the game, but it's definitely against the spirit. There's a strongly worded email in my future.

I pull on my boots, strap on my leather harness, apply a copious amount of insect repellent, and march for the nearest campsite, Campsite D. Everyone should still be asleep, assuming the park ranger hasn't been to this site already. She saw me coming this way, and I had no doubt it was she that stole my phone and knife. She'd save the closest camp to me for last.

Cutting nearly two kilometers through the forest, I step over brush and fallen logs I can barely see in the dim red light from my headlamp. Finally, I reach the edge of the campsite. Four tents are settled amongst the trees, each at least ten meters from another. By the central fire pit, stuck upright in a stump used as a seat, is my red-handled knife. Completely out in the open, there's no way I can sneakily recover my blade.

A quiet snore reaches me on the slow breeze; the park ranger hadn't been here yet, or at least hadn't finished her work. I catch movement among the brush by the far-left tent and flatten myself as a dart thunks into the tree behind where my head had just been. She's here, which I take to mean she's finished her work elsewhere on the island. If she finishes this campsite, my bid to join the fraternity would be completely void. I have to move quickly against her.

Crawling forward, I find a path through the underbrush as the nylon of that tent large enough to sleep seven shimmies and the zipper is undone from the inside. I hate to call the man that steps out "middle-aged," because he looks as old as me. He stumbles a few steps into the poison ivy to relieve himself. The park ranger is watching him too, I knew. She's only a few meters from him, waiting for a moment to strike. Or waiting for me to show myself. I wiggle my blow gun and a dart from my harness and take aim.

"Fuckin' bug..." The man's grumbling tapers as he out pulls the dart with red, fluffy feathers. "What the fuck?" He stares at it for a long breath and I can almost hear the gears grinding in his brain before he drops to a crouch and crawls through the poison ivy. "Mika!" He hisses and slaps the tent's rain fly.

My hand crossbow is loaded and aimed. Slight movement behind the man and I squeeze the trigger, satisfied by the grunt on the other end from a wildly lucky shot. I cock another bolt as the park ranger breaks into a limping sprint away from the campsite. I grab the red handle of my blade as I pass it in pursuit, not giving the middle-aged man a glance as I pass. She weaves through the trees and brush, pausing to rip the bolt from her leg and glare back at me. Despite the injury, she's fast. She knows every patch of uneven ground, every fallen tree in the forest. I keep pace, wary of traps, and recognize the direction she's leading me toward: Campsite A, the farthest from the ferry dock.

If not for the forest of tall beech trees, I would see the sun rising over Lake Michigan as I enter the campsite. Two smaller and one larger tent surround the fire pit and the mangled frame of the larger one lets me know the park ranger had already visited here in the night.

She gasps and trips, twisting to crab walk away from me with a wry grin. "It's my own fault, agent." Blood flows around her fingers where she holds her leg. "I could have ended this hours ago, but my own hubris assured me I could toy around. That I could enjoy myself. I guess it's fitting the Club finally sends someone for me."

I flourish my knife and crouch in front of her. "I know nothing about you, only that I was to stop a known serial. You're my initiation," I say. "I'm not even a full agent yet." I kneel a little closer.

"Well." She winces and spits to her side. "You sure are chatty for a school kid. Are you going to…" She looks down at the river of red down her khaki blouse and up at my knife with a blade to match the handle. "You're fast. What's your name?" Her voice is nothing more than a hoarse breath.

"Brown. Mr. Brown."

* * *

Okay, wow, deep breath…

I thought I was writing this stuff to get out of the mire of dark fantasy and here I just wrote… that… I swear, officer, I've never killed another human. I may have wanted to, but have never taken action or seriously considered taking action. Now, of course, if I had a Deathnote and could cause someone's death by writing their name, that's different…

When I first planned this story, it was totally different. The killer was hoping to murder everyone on the island, only to find someone murdered them first. Lots of fun annoyances, like going to Kroger and they're out of Fruity Pebbles, and you see someone with four boxes in their cart.

Except it's with killing people. I couldn't get myself that deep into a character that stalked and killed groups of friends and family across an island over a single night. I failed at my darkness, but ended up with an origin story for another character.

The funnest tidbit is this story takes place on South Manitou Island, where I'll be camping with friends less than two weeks after I first drafted this.

MEMORIES OF THE FUTURE

I grabbed my phone. 6:54am. Six minutes to my alarm, but my bleary eyes caught the notification on my lock screen.

"Check out these memories from 7 years ago!"

Those always get me. What could I possibly have been doing seven years ago today? What did I ever do in the middle of February? I unlocked my phone and tapped into the gallery of cat photos. Derp, I take a half million shots of my cats a day. I grinned at the pics of Smoochie as a kitten and felt the pang of sadness at seeing Grumper's old, tired eyes. Realizing the date, I wanted to roll over and sleep through the rest of the day. There would be no more pictures of Grumper after those. If only I knew it then, I would have stayed home from work and not left his side all day.

Tears stained my pillow when my alarm went off a minute later. I tossed my phone and threw the sheets aside with a deep sniffle. It was so long ago, but still hurt so much. To anyone that commented about my puffy, red eyes back then with, "Oh, his cat died," I wanted to punch in the dick. No, fuck you, my best friend died.

I showered, shaved, brushed my teeth, and was out the door with a coffee and bagel in hand in under a half-hour.

The Thursday was like any Thursday, where I gave a full twenty percent effort for ten percent pay and five percent respect, with zero percent chance of elevating my life. I spent the time between phone calls scrolling through my photos. Grumper in a Santa costume, Grumper when I tried taking him for a walk, a video of Grumper chattering at a bird outside the window, about nine hundred photos of him on or beside my lap or in my arms. Through the photos and videos, I aged rapidly through my teens, then stayed about the same while Grumper got a little grayer and skinnier.

I got home and Smoochie barely raised her face in greeting. "Love you too, baby girl."

My phone chimed with a notification.

"Check out these memories from -9 years ago!"

I blinked at the typo, but clicked into it. A kitten curled against a fat cat that looked a lot like Smoochie. In another, two bearded guys pressed their cheeks together and held up wine glasses for a selfie. *Did I get someone else's pics?* I scrolled to the next, a shot of a spaghetti dinner, another of cheesecake with two forks, the next and last was a blurry shot of one of the beardos modeling underwear. Someone else's pics or not, no force of nature could stop me from zooming in on that one.

The tiny briefs looked real good and... weird... he had almost the same tattoo as me on the shoulder — a Legend of Zelda Triforce — and a few more. They looked amazing on his chiseled pecs and flat stomach. I focused on his other tattoos: two cat paws and... and... Grumper. I frantically zoomed until the photo would zoom no more. Despite the artistic license taken, I recognized that shot of Grumper in a Santa hat tattooed on this stranger's chest.

"What the fuck?" I swiped to the guy's face and ran to the bathroom to hold the phone beside the mirror. I covered his beard with a finger and dropped my phone behind the toilet. I fell back against the wall and slid to the ground as Smoochie started crying for dinner. I stared at the phone behind my toilet, working up the nerve to reach with trembling fingers and open the photo of the two guys again. Unless I had some doppelgänger from another dimension hanging around, there was no denying the one on the left was me. *Who the fuck is the other guy? What the actual fuck is going on here?* I studied the other man's face, noticing the smile lines crinkling the corners of his sky-blue eyes and wondered what effort he put into maintaining that great hair.

I hit the back button in my photo app to bring up the list of memories going out to -29 years from now. *Why not more? I'll only be 50 then.* My finger hovered over that last entry as sweat beaded across my forehead. My breath couldn't come fast enough. There seemed to be no oxygen left in the room. *Shit or get off the pot,* came my grandfather's voice, and I tapped.

The screen went black for the longest second of my life before glowing with the manufacturer's name. I didn't understand for a moment until my lock screen stared back at me. The damn phone crashed and restarted. I frantically went back into my photos and the memories tab, difficult to do with sweaty fingers that the touchscreen didn't want to register. It went back 16 years, but nothing into the future.

Smoochie still howled, but I ignored her as I grabbed the sink counter to pull myself up and in front of the mirror. I rubbed my smooth cheek and wondered what I'd look like with a beard. I pulled off my shirt and patted the sides of my gut, imagining myself as I saw in that photo; lean, muscular, hot. Happy. Possibly in love.

It had to have been a fever dream brought on by my grief. I fed Smoochie so she could continue her evening of ignoring my existence and found myself staring at the takeout ads spread across the kitchen island. Pizza, Chinese, Italian, more pizza, yet more pizza. I pushed a sheet aside and saw an ad for a kickboxing gym announcing its grand opening only a block away. I looked closer at the low res image of a bearded man beside the logo throwing a jab.

A very familiar bearded man with sky-blue eyes and an easy smile.

AND LO, THE ANGEL

"I have no room in my inn, but you may stay in my stables with my donkeys and sheep and goats and cows and chickens out back."

Mrs. Peters mouthed the words as third-grade Johnny Winters nearly screamed them in a single breath.

"We thank you," mumbled Evan Chan and Johnny pushed his door stage right with the help of two classmates that couldn't remember enough lines to land a part.

Kelly Bobson waddled forward, rubbing the padding across her belly. "I must have this child, Joseph! I simply must!"

Mrs. Peters frowned at the overacting and dramatic way Kelly threw an arm across her forehead. Four kids dressed as barn animals entered from stage right pushing a hay bale and cutout painted as a hay pile.

"Oh, Joseph, I simply must have this baby right now!" Kelly moaned and swooned onto the hay bale.

Evan reached behind it and held the doll up for the audience to see. "Jesus is born," he said with his eyes directed at his feet.

"He wasn't this bad at rehearsal," Mrs. Peters whispered to herself.

Three wisemen shuffled in to lay their gifts beside where Kelly held the baby Jesus, rocking him far more animatedly than a newborn should be rocked. Mrs. Peters pulled the flask from her back pocket, finding strength in grandma's medicine.

"And lo, the angel of the lord appears," said Melchior, played by Allen Horne.

Mrs. Peters wrung her hands with nervous anticipation. She could make out the white of Charlotte Olson's costume high on the catwalk and waited with bated breath for her to be lowered into the scene. It had taken a mountain of permission slips and a half dozen school board meetings for this to be allowed, but Mrs. Peters saw this at the pageant her sister directed last year and would not be outdone by that smug bitch.

"Um… And lo, the angel of the lord appears," Allen repeated.

"What the hell, Frank? Lower her!" Mrs. Peters spat through gritted teeth.

The auditorium exploded with the light of a

thousand suns, blinding all that looked upon the pageant. The room erupted with gasps and cries of pain or shock. Mrs. Peters rubbed her eyes and blinked until she could look upon the angel.

Three wheels of pure gold circled a central eye that seared into the soul and beyond anything it looked upon. Four feathered wings spread to almost the full width of the auditorium, but their slow movement alone was not enough to keep it aloft in a gleaming beam of pure sunlight.

"BEHOLD, I HAVE COME." Mrs. Peters fell to her knees with the voice that threatened to rupture her mind, to shatter her sanity, yet she could not look away. Evan Chan, playing the part of Joseph, fell with blood streaming from his ears and eyes. "LOOK UPON ME AND DESPAIR." The audience moaned and clawed at their ears and faces, but none possessed the will to stand or flee.

The angel remained in place over the audience for a long moment with no one capable of responding to it. Mrs. Peters felt her mind cracking under the infinite gaze of that single eye and began to understand the depth of her inconsequential life. She felt her sanity as a physical object in her mind crumbling to dust in an instant or an eternity when met with a being so incomprehensibly beyond that which her mortal frame could understand.

Everything that was her would shatter in another fraction of an instant in the angel's presence, yet if she survived, she would never truly live after gazing upon the absolute beauty and symmetry of its geometry.

* * *

"What the hell happened here?" Senior Detective McClacky flicked away his cigarette butt and passed three officers retching into the bushes beside the auditorium doors. Another sat hugging her knees and gently rocking while staring into the space before her.

"It's a bloodbath, sir," said the officer walking beside him. "Seven years on the force and I've never heard of anything like this. Over a hundred victims killed themselves, each other, or seemed to have gone from shock."

"Goddamn. Of course when I'm two weeks from retirement. No survivors?"

"Only one, the principal's wife. Mrs. Peters."

She sat between two medics, hugging a shiny shock blanket around her shoulders and mumbling to herself.

"What is she saying?" McClacky asked.

"And lo, the angel of the lord appears," said the

other detective.

McClacky jumped back with a gasp as Mrs. Peters looked up at him. Her face was ashen and clammy, but her eyes... Her eyes were a ruin of red pulp, as if pecked out by greedy crows.

"And lo, the angel of the lord appears!"

COLD SNAP

Last one. This deserves a brief introduction, as it stands out. It's not weird or funny. It's not really anything at all. My challenge was to write a scene about two people keeping each other warm, involving love, but also without over-describing the scene, as I have been accused of doing. What I came up with is a story with an ambiguous narrator. I hope it makes you feel chilly.

* * *

"I thought you were the great outdoorsman." I blew into my trembling fingers. If it helped at all, my hands were too numb to tell the difference.

"The wood's too wet," Josh said and sat beside me on the log. "And *I* never said anything about being an outdoorsman. *You* bestowed that honorific upon me yesterday when I got the fire going after an hour of failure."

"We should go to the ranger's station," I said around chattering teeth.

Josh looked up at the moonless sky and back to me. I could barely see where his beard ended and the rest of his face started in the starlight. Neither of us needed to say it. Without a flashlight, we'd never make it three miles through the woods to the ranger station. We were woefully unprepared for camping at all, much less with a cold snap gripping the island.

"Maybe we'd be better in the tent. At least it would trap some heat." Josh nodded his chin toward the canvas mess I spent hours erecting yesterday while he built a fire.

Josh stood and slipped his hand into mine as he did. It felt like fire, but might have only been a single degree warmer. He pulled aside the main flap and entered just behind me into complete darkness. We blindly maneuvered in the tight space, finding our own sleeping bags and pulling off our heavy boots. My toes were as numb as my fingers, but rubbing them restored some sense of life. After a moment, I realized my wool socks were damp, and I pulled those off as well.

"I almost don't want to get into the sleeping bag," Josh chuckled. I could hear the tremble in his voice so close to me. "No wonder I'm freezing. Everything is wet." His overcoat rustled as he worked his way out of it. "Where did we put the spare clothes?"

"Our packs are out there, hanging in a tree somewhere." I fumbled at the zipper of my coat. I don't know what noise of frustration I made, but Josh was touching my jacket a moment later, feeling for the zipper, and undoing it for me. "Thank you," I mumbled and realized how large Josh's presence felt in the tent. Without light, he could be anywhere beside me, and my mind filled every crevice with him. Every inhale brought with it the mix of our unwashed bodies, overshadowed by a lingering hint of Josh's beard oil. My thermals were damp from a day hiking on the humid island. It clung to my skin as I pulled it over my head, and the chill air immediately attacked the bare skin. Despite that, I hadn't realized how uncomfortable the moist fabric had been until I was free of it.

Josh shuffled beside me, grazing his back against my arm. "Can't find the top of my damn bag," he mumbled as much to himself as to me.

"You're not sleeping in wet jeans, are you?" I asked and focused on the button of mine. After that, there was a zipper, and I prayed I wouldn't need Josh's help there. Since undergrad, we hadn't spent more than a week apart and had gotten into more trouble than I wanted to remember. *Someone with two doctorates and a mountain of published works doesn't need someone else's help to get out of their own pants.* I realized how that sounded even as I thought it. I loved Josh. He was the only man I ever loved. But not like *that.* Why did helping me when my hands were too frozen have to mean anything? Why was I making this weird? We've seen each other undressed plenty of times, mostly by accident, a few times not. We've helped each other out of our pants plenty of times over the years. Maybe it was the complete darkness baffling my mind.

"My goddamn thermals are all soaked too," Josh grumbled and rustled beside me. I managed my own jeans' button, and to my relief and embarrassment, the fly was already down. I made a mental note to not wear denim camping again. It soaked up every drop of dew I brushed past and would never dry. The heat generated by our struggles to disrobe in the tight space helped cut the dread chill as I shoved my wet things into a corner and tried to find the head of my sleeping bag.

"Jesus fuck!" Josh grunted. "It's a fucking glacier in this thing."

I slipped a leg into my bag and repeated his curse.

"Get your ass in here with me," Josh said.

I laughed around my shiver. "There's barely enough room for one of us."

"You're the engineer. Can't we zipper these together?"

I nodded, though he couldn't see it. "You're as smart as you are bearded."

We played an awkward game of Twister, not that any game of Twister isn't awkward, for seven minutes in the complete dark, trying to unzip the bags and merge them. Josh was everywhere in the tent, his bare skin burning under mine every time we grazed against each other. By the time he declared success, the tent was almost comfortable.

I pushed into the double sleeping bag, cocooning myself in cold cotton. My body heat leeched into the fabric as Josh slid in to my left. We lay there a moment in silence, shoulders and thighs touching in the tight space while our bodies regained something like life.

For the first time in hours, I felt like my life wasn't about to end that night. I sighed up at the canvas a few feet overhead. "If I'm going to freeze to death tonight, I'm glad to be doing it next to you."

"Yeah, me too, Rye." He laughed and floundered for my hand, giving it a squeeze. "If the ranger has to find my blue corpse next to any other blue corpse, at least it'll be yours."

Josh still held my left hand when I lurched, rolling in place to face him with my right hand resting against his shoulder. I could see nothing but imagined the creases at the corners of his dark eyes and dimples when he smiled.

"I have an idea," Josh said and let go of my left hand. He took my right and lurch-rolled away from me before pressing his back against my chest and squeezing my arm into his whorls of chest hair. I adjusted myself to maximize skin contact. I may not be a thermal engineer, but I knew enough to minimize heat loss.

"Was this your idea?" My nose was close to the nape of Josh's neck.

"Yeah, but also, let's never go camping again." He chuckled and raised my hand to kiss it. "Good night, River. In case we do die, know that I love you."

I bit back my grin, pushed my forehead against him, and kissed the back of his neck. "I love you too, Beards." Cold snaps forgotten, the sleeping bag felt as warm as summer when I squeezed him tight in a single-armed hug.

DETERMINATION

*Tchotchkes.

From the Author

I've been yammering throughout this and I'm not sure I have more to say at this point. Obviously — or not too obviously — thank you for sticking out to the end. The first chapter was rife with lies, suggesting this book is the product of a month challenge. By the time I'm done with editing, it'll be closer to four months. That's about how long *Necromancer of Urbus* took, and that was a full novel two and half times longer that went through professional editing. None of that matters to you. Point is, writing's hard, but I love it. I've done it a few other times, check it out:

The Chronicler's Awakening Trilogy:
- Realms of Terswood
- Trials of Throk'tar
- Seeds of Farsil
- Necromancer of Urbus (prequel)

Collections:
- Ooo Shiny! Volume 1

About the Author

I've enjoyed writing most of my life, but it took a global pandemic to get me focused at home and dust off the terrible old fan fiction I wrote in high school. I promptly dumped that in the trash and wrote *Realms of Terswood*. I write in the hours I can find between full time work as a programmer, training and teaching taekwondo, and some vague attempt to remain social with friends. My husband and our cats live in Michigan.

My Mailing list

Get free stories, writing updates, find out about upcoming events, and chances for advance book readings. Scan this QR code with your phone and follow the link.

Made in the USA
Columbia, SC
09 January 2023

75225931R00070